"Who is talking back there?" called Mrs. Rumford

Everyone got quiet.

Mrs. Rumford walked back toward Liza and Bridget. "Were you the ones who were talking?"

Liza looked at her shoes.

Bridget didn't answer either.

"I cannot have this noise in the halls," said Mrs. Rumford. "Both of you will walk quietly downstairs. Then you may come back up again. You can meet the rest of us in our room."

Liza and Bridget turned around. They started back down the stairs.

"And," said Mrs. Rumford, "I don't want to hear a peep from either one of you. Not a single peep." Mrs. Rumford closed the stairwell door.

"Peep," said Liza very quietly. "Peep, peep."

"Peep," answered Bridget, not so quietly.

And then they were both peeping and laughing at the same time.

OTHER CHAPTER BOOKS FROM PUFFIN

Third Grade Is Terrible

Barbara Baker

illustrated by Roni Shepherd

PUFFIN BOOKS

for Lucia Monfried
B. A. B.

for my wonderful son,
Morgan
R. S.

PUFFIN BOOKS
Published by the Penguin Group
Penguin Putnam Books for Young Readers,
345 Hudson Street, New York, New York 10014, U.S.A.
Penguin Books Ltd, 27 Wrights Lane, London W8 5TZ, England
Penguin Books Australia Ltd, Ringwood, Victoria, Australia
Penguin Books Canada Ltd, 10 Alcorn Avenue, Toronto, Ontario, Canada M4V 3B2
Penguin Books (N.Z.) Ltd, 182-190 Wairau Road, Auckland 10, New Zealand

Penguin Books Ltd, Registered Offices: Harmondsworth, Middlesex, England

First published in the United States of America by E. P. Dutton,
a division of NAL Penguin Inc., 1989
Published by Puffin Books,
a member of Penguin Putnam Books for Young Readers, 1999

20 19 18 17 16 15 14

THE LIBRARY OF CONGRESS HAS CATALOGED THE E. P. DUTTON EDITION AS FOLLOWS:
Baker, Barbara.
Third grade is terrible / by Barbara Baker; illustrated by Roni Shepherd.
   p. cm.
Summary: Liza is convinced third grade is going to be great until she gets
to school that first day and everything starts going wrong.
ISBN 0-525-44425-4
[1. Schools—Fiction. 2. Friendship—Fiction.] I. Shepherd, Roni, ill. II. Title.
PZ7.B16922Th 1988 [E]—dc19 88-3631 CIP AC

Puffin Books ISBN 0-14-130103-1

Printed in the United States of America

RL: 2.9

BARBARA BAKER is a former elementary-school teacher and the author of *The William Problem*. Ms. Baker's other books include *Digby and Kate*, *Digby and Kate Again*, *N-O Spells No!* and *Oh, Emma!* She lives in New York City.

RONI SHEPHERD is a freelance illustrator. She lives in San Francisco, California.

1

Liza Farmer pushed the back of her spoon into her oatmeal. Milk rushed in to fill up the hole.

"Liza," said her mother. "Stop playing with your breakfast."

The oatmeal is the beach, Liza said to herself, and the milk is the ocean. She made another little hole. She could almost see the ocean rushing in to fill up her footprints in the sand. The warm sun, the blue sky, the water tickling her toes . . .

"Liza!" said Mrs. Farmer.

Liza picked up her spoon.

No more beaches. Not until next summer.

1

But that was okay. Today was the first day of school. And third grade was going to be great. Liza put some oatmeal into her mouth. "Yuck," she said.

"I *like* oatmeal," said her little sister Peggy. She took a big spoonful so her mother could see.

"You *would*," said Liza. "You're only five."

"I like it too," said Edward, "and I'm going into the sixth grade."

"So what," said Liza. "Third grade is going to be great!" She took another bite of oatmeal. That Edward. Just because he was a few years older than she was, he thought he knew everything.

"Third grade is terrible," said Edward. "Really terrible."

"Edward," said Mrs. Farmer, "that's enough."

Liza didn't say anything. She was sorry that summer vacation was over. School could never be as good as the beach. But she knew that third grade was going to be great for *her*.

When Edward was in third grade he had had Mrs. Rumford. She made the class work, work, work. There was no time for fun! Mrs. Rumford was mean.

But Liza was getting Mrs. Lane. She was the best teacher in the whole school. Her class always had parties for holidays and birthdays. They got to go on lots of trips, too. They went to the library once a week. Liza loved to read library books.

And Mrs. Lane was pretty.

Liza had a new dress on, and almost-new sneakers. She would comb her hair and put a barrette in it. Then Mrs. Lane would see that she was pretty too. Well, at least not ugly.

Liza sighed. She twisted a strand of short, straight hair around her finger. Why had she let her mother talk her into a summer haircut? Her best friend Heather's hair was long. Really long. It looked great. Liza pulled at her hair. Grow, she thought. Grow fast.

"Liza, you're not eating," said her mother. "And Heather will be here any minute. You know you have to be more responsible this year. I have to get Peggy ready for school."

"I'm a big girl," said Peggy. "I'm going to school."

"You're just a kindergarten ba—"

"Liza!" said her mother.

"Okay, okay," said Liza. She took a last bite of oatmeal, gulped her orange juice, and pushed her chair away from the table.

Edward was finished too. He dumped his dishes into the sink. "Bye, Mom," he called, heading for the front door. "I'm going to meet the guys at school."

"Remember," he yelled to Liza, "third grade is *terrible*." The door slammed.

"Mom," said Liza, "Edward—"

"I know. I know," said Mrs. Farmer. "But he's gone. Where's the comb, Liza? I've got to comb Peggy's hair. And you need to comb yours. And please let the dog in."

Liza could hear Chester barking in the backyard. Where was that comb? Maybe in

4

the bathroom. Maybe upstairs. Maybe she could use her father's hairbrush.

The doorbell rang. Liza ran to answer it.

"Liza, come here," yelled her mother.

Liza ran back to the kitchen. "It's Heather," she said. "She's waiting outside. I've got to go."

"Then here's a kiss for luck," said her mother. She kissed Liza and gave her a hug. "I'll see you after school. Have a good first day."

Chester was still barking. Mrs. Farmer ran to let him in.

"*I'll* see you *in* school," said Peggy. "I'm a big—"

"Pain in the neck," finished Liza as she ran out of the kitchen and through the living room. She scooped up her backpack and her lunch box. She had the feeling that she was forgetting something. Something important. But what? She had her lunch box, and her notebook and pencil were in her backpack. Her sneakers were tied and her socks matched. She pulled the front door open. Whatever it was, it was too late now.

Third grade was going to be great!

2

The schoolyard was crowded. It looked as if about a million kids had gotten there before Liza and Heather.

"Look," said Liza. She pointed to a group of third-grade girls in a corner. The third-grade boys were running all over the place.

Liza and Heather made their way over to the other girls.

Everyone was talking at the same time. Liza looked around to see who was dressed up for the first day. Everybody. Too bad. She wanted to be the only one. Except for Heather, of course. She could be dressed up, too, since they were best friends. Heather always looked

8

nice anyway. That was just the way Heather was.

"Hey, Liza," said Monica Marks.

Liza was surprised to hear Monica call her. Monica hadn't liked her last year. She was stuck-up.

"Hey, Liza," Monica said again. "Why didn't you comb your hair?"

Now everyone looked at Liza. She felt herself getting red. Her hair! That was what she had forgotten. And she didn't have a comb or a barrette. How could she do such a dumb thing?

Monica patted her own smooth ponytail. "Don't worry," she said. "Your hair is so short it doesn't look *too* bad." Monica smiled—a mean smile.

Liza wanted to punch her. She wanted to pull that smooth ponytail hard.

A whistle blew three times. "Line up," called Mrs. Ross, the principal. She put her whistle to her lips and blew one more time.

"Ross the boss," said Monica. "Let's go."

She began to run across the yard. Her ponytail bounced up and down.

"Come on, Liza," said Heather. "Your hair looks okay."

"It does not," said Liza. But she started walking. "I hate that stupid Monica," she said. "I hate her." But Heather wasn't listening. She was rushing ahead.

Soon the whole school was lined up, class by class. All except for the kindergarten kids. They always went right to their classrooms.

"Look," said Heather. "Our class is the biggest."

Liza was trying to comb her hair with her fingers. She looked. It was true. Their line *was* a little longer than the other third grade. Maybe some kids from last year moved away when they found out they were getting Mrs. Rumford. Maybe they begged their parents to send them to another school.

The kids in Mrs. Rumford's line didn't look happy. Poor them, thought Liza. Lucky us. She looked up at Mrs. Lane.

Mrs. Lane was counting. She pointed to each kid in the class as she counted. Then she wrote something down on a piece of paper. "I need a helper," she said.

Liza's hand shot up fast.

"Okay," said Mrs. Lane. She pointed to Liza. "What's your name?"

"Elizabeth Farmer," said Liza. "But everyone calls me Liza."

"All right, Liza, would you please take this note to Mrs. Ross's office? Then you can meet the rest of us in the classroom."

"Yes, Mrs. Lane," said Liza. She took the piece of paper Mrs. Lane held out. Mrs. Lane had long fingernails with pink polish. Even her hands are pretty, thought Liza. And *I* am her first helper.

Liza looked at Monica. Monica made a face. Heather didn't look too friendly either.

Jealous, said Liza to herself. They're just jealous. Then she turned around and headed for the side door. She hoped Heather would save her a good seat.

The first graders were already coming into the school. Liza held her note up and pushed her way through.

When she got to the office, she had to wait.

Miss Horn, the secretary, was typing. Liza stood by her desk, looking around. Some kids were sitting on chairs. And some parents too. She didn't know who the kids were. They must be new.

One girl looked as if she might be a third grader. She was about the right size. Her hair was even shorter than Liza's, and she was wearing jeans. She was chewing a fingernail. Probably nervous, thought Liza. And she'll be even more nervous if she does turn out to be a third grader. Mrs. Lane's class was bigger, so a new kid would get Mrs. Rumford for sure. Too bad for her, Liza thought. She must be dumb anyway. Everyone knew you didn't wear jeans the first day of school.

The girl stopped chewing on her fingernail. She saw Liza watching her. "Hi," she said. She smiled.

Just then Mrs. Ross came in. The whistle was hanging on a chain around her neck. Her gray hair looked a little messy. "I see we have a full house," she said.

The new kids didn't say anything.

Liza said, "I have a note from Mrs. Lane." She felt very important. It was great to be a helper the very first day of school.

Mrs. Ross read the note. "Hmmm," she said. She frowned. "Please tell Mrs. Lane I'll be in to see her as soon as I can."

"Yes, Mrs. Ross," said Liza. She walked quietly out of the office. She would show the principal what a good helper she was.

As soon as Liza was in the hall, she started to run. She ran all the way down the hall and up the stairs to her new classroom.

Good thing there aren't any monitors yet, she thought. It would be terrible to get reported for running before she even got to her room. She didn't want to get into any trouble this year. She wanted third grade to be perfect.

3

Liza pushed open the door to Mrs. Lane's class.

Everybody looked. Mrs. Lane said, "So here you are, Liza. Did you give the note to Mrs. Ross?"

"Yes," said Liza. "She said she'd be in soon to see you."

"Thank you," said Mrs. Lane. "You've been a big help." She smiled at Liza. She had a beautiful smile. Her pink lipstick matched her fingernails. Her teeth were a little crooked.

Liza ran her tongue over her own straight teeth. Maybe if she pushed them a little every day, they'd get crooked. It was worth a try.

15

She knew her mother would never let her wear lipstick.

"Liza," Mrs. Lane said. "We have a little problem here."

Liza stopped pushing her teeth. She looked up.

"That's what the note was about," Mrs. Lane said.

Now the whole class was listening.

"You see," said Mrs. Lane, "there are not enough desks in this room for all of you."

Liza looked around—not one empty desk. She saw Heather and Monica sitting together. The rats.

"So," Mrs. Lane said, "would you please sit at the reading table until we get a desk for you?"

That wasn't so bad, thought Liza. Maybe she would even get a *new* desk. Maybe there was a shiny new desk in the storeroom right now.

Liza smiled at Mrs. Lane to let her know she didn't mind sitting at the reading table.

She wanted her to see what a good sport she was.

Everyone was watching her. Liza walked to the back of the room. The reading table was in the corner. It was big and round and empty.

Liza put her backpack and lunch box on the floor. She put her notebook and pencil in the middle of the table. She had plenty of room.

Some shelves with science and art supplies were in back of her. And she could see what was going on in the whole room from here. Not bad at all. It was probably the best seat in the room.

Some of the kids were still twisting around in their seats to look at her. She wanted to give Monica and Heather a dirty look. But Mrs. Lane clapped her hands.

"All right, class, let's get back to business."

Everyone faced front.

Mrs. Lane started talking about all the things they would be doing in third grade. Liza

looked around the room. It was great to see all of her friends again.

Mrs. Lane was just getting to the good part, about class trips, when the door opened. It was the principal. "Good morning, third graders," she said.

Mrs. Lane went over to the door. "Please be patient, everyone. I have to talk to Mrs. Ross for a few minutes." Then they went out into the hall. Mrs. Lane left the door open. Everyone waited quietly.

When they came back in, Mrs. Lane said, "Class, you know that this room is too crowded." Everyone looked around. "So," she said, "Mrs. Ross and I have decided that it will be better if one of you goes into the other third-grade room. Then both classes will be just about the same size."

All of a sudden the room got very quiet. Most of the kids looked down at their desks or out the window. They didn't want the principal to notice them.

But Liza knew she was safe. After all, she

was Mrs. Lane's first helper. Mrs. Lane must like her. Liza looked right at Mrs. Ross and smiled.

Mrs. Ross smiled back. "Elizabeth Farmer," she said. "You're a good helper. I'm sure you wouldn't mind helping us now. Will you bring your things and come with me?"

4

Mrs. Ross made a mistake, thought Liza. She doesn't really mean me. She couldn't.

But all the kids had turned around again to stare at Liza. And Mrs. Ross and Mrs. Lane were looking at her too.

Liza picked up her things. She walked to the front of the room. Her whole body felt stiff. She did not look at Heather. She did not look at anybody. She knew if she did, she would start to cry—right there in front of everyone.

Liza waited for Mrs. Ross. I will talk to her in the hall, she thought. I will tell her she made a mistake. Then she will let me come right back into Mrs. Lane's room.

Liza followed the principal into the hall. "Mrs. Ross," she said in a small voice, "I think you—"

Mrs. Ross didn't hear her. She was already headed for Mrs. Rumford's room. "Elizabeth," she said, "I'm sure you will like being in Mrs. Rumford's room. Your brother had Mrs. Rumford in the third grade, and he did very well that year. I think it will be a good class for you."

Liza wanted to say, "Edward hated Mrs. Rumford, and I will too," but Mrs. Ross did not give her a chance. She just kept telling Liza about how wonderful third grade was going to be.

Liza hurried to keep up with the principal. Mrs. Rumford's room was at the far end of the hall.

"And," said Mrs. Ross, "I'm so glad you didn't mind changing classes."

"But—" said Liza. "Mrs. Ross, I—"

"Yes, dear," said the principal. But she kept walking.

"Mrs. Ross—I have to go to the bathroom."

"Oh." Mrs. Ross stopped. "Can you wait?"

"No," said Liza. "It's an emergency."

"Well, hurry then, dear. I have a lot to do this morning."

Liza ran into the bathroom. She knew she had to think of something fast, or it would be too late. She looked at herself in the spotty mirror over the sink. Her face was red. Her hair was a mess. No wonder Mrs. Lane doesn't want me, she said to herself. But *I* want Mrs. Lane.

Just then Liza got a great idea. She would say that her *mother* wanted her to be in Mrs. Lane's class. That would work. Mothers were more important to principals than children.

Liza ran into a bathroom stall. She flushed the toilet for the principal to hear. Then she rushed out the door to tell Mrs. Ross about why she really had to stay in Mrs. Lane's room.

Mrs. Ross was not there.

Liza looked down the hall. There she was, right at the door to Mrs. Rumford's room. Please wait, thought Liza. Please don't open the door. But just as Liza got there, the principal pushed the door open and went in. Liza had to follow.

Mrs. Ross said, "Here is a new student for your class, Mrs. Rumford. Her name is Elizabeth Farmer." She gave some papers to Mrs. Rumford. Then she turned and walked quickly out of the room.

Mrs. Rumford said, "We are glad to have you with us, Elizabeth." But she did not look glad at all.

Liza looked around her. Everyone had a notebook open. Working already. There was a big sign on one bulletin board, NEATNESS COUNTS. There were a few ugly fall pictures, too. On the blackboard she saw CLASS RULES printed in big letters. And there were about a hundred rules that took up the whole board.

"We are all putting these rules in the front

of our notebooks," said Mrs. Rumford. "You will have to work quickly, Elizabeth, to catch up."

Liza looked at Mrs. Rumford. "Everyone calls me Liza," she said.

"In *this* room," said Mrs. Rumford, "we will call you Elizabeth. We do not use nicknames."

"But Mrs. Rumford," said Liza. "I—"

"Yes, Elizabeth? What is it?"

"Mrs. Rumford, I . . . I have to go to the bathroom."

"Later," said Mrs. Rumford.

5

There were two empty seats in the back of the room. Liza headed for the one near the window.

"Elizabeth," said Mrs. Rumford, "please take the desk next to William Spear."

Liza sat down next to William. She tried not to look at him. He was the biggest creep in the whole third grade. He was skinny. He was as skinny as a spear. And his nose was red. William always had a tissue in his hand. And when he wasn't blowing his nose, he was sniffing.

Liza looked around. She knew most of the kids in the class. But they were not her

friends. Her friends were in Mrs. Lane's class.

Liza took a quick look at William. He was writing with one hand and wiping his nose with the other. Disgusting. Liza looked away.

The desk on the other side of her was the empty one. She wished she could sit there.

Amy Cutter sat right in front of her. Amy was pretty, but she acted a lot like Monica Marks. Stuck-up. Maybe this year would be different, thought Liza. Maybe Amy would be her friend.

Just then Amy turned around. "Ha ha," she whispered. "You got Rumford, too." Then she smiled a mean smile—just like Monica.

Liza stuck her tongue out. But she was too late. Amy had already turned around.

Liza reached out and poked Amy with her pencil.

"Ow!" said Amy. She said it in a loud voice.

Mrs. Rumford looked up. "What's going on back there?" She frowned.

"*Elizabeth* poked me," whined Amy. "And I was just doing my work."

"Elizabeth," said Mrs. Rumford. "This is not the way to start the new year."

"I only wanted to borrow a pencil," said Liza.

"And what is that in your hand?" asked Mrs. Rumford.

"Uh," said Liza. She quickly covered the pencil point with her finger. "This one is broken."

"Elizabeth," said Mrs. Rumford. "In third grade we come to school with two sharp pencils every day. In third grade we come to school ready to work. Do you understand?"

"Yes," said Liza.

"Good," said Mrs. Rumford. "Now, I want you to settle down and work. You may sharpen your pencil later."

"But—" said Liza.

"William Spear," said Mrs. Rumford. "Do you have an extra pencil?"

William took a pencil from his pencil case. He held it out to Liza.

Liza didn't want to touch it. It was probably wet. It probably had a million wet germs on it. But Mrs. Rumford was watching. So was Amy Cutter.

"I just remembered," said Liza. "I think I have an extra pencil in my backpack."

William put his pencil away. Liza put her pencil in her backpack and then pulled it out again. "Yes," she said, "I do."

Everybody started working again. Except for Liza. She put CLASS RULES on the top of her page. Then she looked out the window.

She wondered what the kids were doing in Mrs. Lane's class. Probably something that was fun. She thought about Heather and the others. If only she could be there too. If only she could be anywhere except here. Like maybe the beach . . .

"Elizabeth . . . Elizabeth!"

Someone was calling her. It was Mrs. Rumford.

"Elizabeth, I am glad to see that you have time for looking out the window," she said. "I hope this means you have finished your work."

Liza didn't say anything. She looked down at her empty page.

"I would like to see your notebook," said Mrs. Rumford. "Please bring it up here."

Liza closed her notebook. She stood up.

Just then the door opened. Liza sat down fast. She was safe. At least for now. The principal came into the room, and she had the new girl with her. The girl from the office. The one with short hair and jeans.

Mrs. Ross smiled. "Good morning, everyone. We have a new student. Her name is Bridget Duffy, and I know you will all make her feel welcome."

Bridget started chewing a fingernail.

Mrs. Ross gave Bridget's papers to Mrs.

Rumford. "Don't forget," she told her, "Welcome Assembly in ten minutes."

"Thank you," said Mrs. Rumford. "We'll be there."

As soon as the principal was gone, Mrs. Rumford said, "Bridget, you will sit next to Elizabeth." She pointed to the empty seat. "Please hurry and put your things away. We must all get ready to go to assembly."

Everyone watched Bridget walk to the back of the room.

"And Elizabeth," said Mrs. Rumford.

Everyone turned to look at Liza.

"You may go to the girls' room now," said Mrs. Rumford. "But be quick about it."

Liza planned to be as slow about it as she could. She didn't want Mrs. Rumford to remember about her notebook before assembly.

Liza took tiny little steps down the hall. She pushed open the girls' room door. She still

didn't have to use the toilet, but she needed something to do for ten minutes.

Liza looked around. Not much here. She pressed the button on the liquid soap dispenser. A thin stream of smelly green soap oozed out.

She put some soap on the end of her finger.

Now what?

She looked around. The mirror. Liza didn't even think about what she did next.

Just as she finished writing I HATE MRS. RUMFORD in big soapy letters on the mirror, she heard the bathroom door start to open. Liza froze.

"Elizabeth? Are you in there?"

6

"Elizabeth?"

Liza stared at the bathroom door.

A head peeked around.

It was the new girl, Bridget Duffy.

"What are you doing here?" yelled Liza. "You shouldn't sneak up on a person like that."

Bridget came in and closed the door. "I didn't sneak up on you. I had to go to the bathroom. Mrs. Rumford said to tell you—" Bridget stopped. She looked at the mirror.

"I didn't do it," said Liza.

"Don't worry," Bridget said. "I won't tell."

36

"Good," said Liza. She was sorry she had yelled at Bridget. She was sorry she had said, "I didn't do it." That was a dumb thing to say.

"Will you wait for me?" Bridget asked. "The rest of the class went to the auditorium. I don't know where it is."

"I'll wait," said Liza. She took some paper towels. She wiped the mirror. It was a big mess.

"I'm ready," said Bridget. "Let's go."

Downstairs they stopped to look in the kindergarten.

"Those little kids are cute," said Bridget.

"Not all of them," said Liza. "My sister is in there. She thinks she's wonderful. But she's just a pain." Peggy was painting a picture at the easel. It was green and messy. It looked like the bathroom mirror upstairs. "We better go," said Liza.

The auditorium was full. All the classes were there except for the kindergarten.

Liza looked for Mrs. Rumford's class.

"There. I see them near the front," she told Bridget. She started down the aisle. Bridget followed her.

Someone reached out and hit Liza on the leg. It was Edward.

"Who was that big kid?" Bridget asked. "The one who hit you?" Bridget sounded nervous.

"Don't worry," said Liza. "That's just my stupid brother, Edward. He always does things like that."

"Hurry up, girls," said Mrs. Rumford. She pointed to two empty seats right next to her.

Liza looked back before she sat down. Edward was watching her and Mrs. Rumford. At first he looked surprised. Then he started to laugh. He put his hands up to his neck and made a choking face. He knew she had Mrs. Rumford.

I'll get him, thought Liza. She stuck her tongue out at Edward.

"Elizabeth!" said Mrs. Rumford.

Liza crashed into her seat.

The principal came out on the stage. "Good morning, everyone," she said in a cheerful voice. "It's so nice to see you all again. I just know we're going to have a wonderful year."

"Blah, blah, blah," said Liza softly. She heard Bridget giggle. Mrs. Rumford frowned.

Liza looked around. She saw Mrs. Lane's class on the other side of the auditorium. Heather was in the front row. Liza wished she could be sitting next to Heather. She looked at Mrs. Rumford. Wonderful year? No way!

When assembly was over, Mrs. Rumford led the class back upstairs. "Five more minutes to finish copying rules," she said. "Then we go to music. Those people who are not finished on time will stay in during recess."

Liza opened her notebook. She started writing as fast as she could. She zipped through those rules. She hadn't written this much the whole summer.

"Close your books," Mrs. Rumford said. "Line up."

Liza slammed her book shut. She had finished just in time.

The rest of the day was bad. Music was the same old songs. Math was dumb worksheets. Social studies was boring.

And lunch was the worst of all. Heather and the other kids from Mrs. Lane's class were sitting together. They looked happy. Heather waved and smiled at Liza. Then she went back to talking with Monica Marks.

Liza was the last one at her table. She had to sit across from William Spear. How could anyone eat a tuna fish sandwich sitting across from William?

Liza tried not to look at him, but she could hear. Sniff, blow, chew. . . . Sniff, blow, chew. . . . Yuck.

She put her sandwich back in her lunch box. Maybe she would eat it later. Maybe Heather

41

could come over after school. They could have a snack together.

Liza was hungry all afternoon. She kept thinking about the sandwich in her lunch box. But there was no way she could eat it now.

Finally it was almost time to go home.

"Open your notebooks, class," said Mrs. Rumford. "I am coming around to check your work."

Mrs. Rumford had a red pencil in her hand. She stopped at every desk. "Very neat," she said to Nancy Higgins. "Work slower next time," she told James Rich. She did not say anything to Joseph Russo or Michael Green or Sara Port.

Liza waited for her turn. When Mrs. Rumford got to Amy Cutter she said, "Good work, Amy."

Liza was next. She knew that Mrs. Rumford would not say "good work" to her. Her work was a big mess.

42

Mrs. Rumford stopped. She looked at Liza's notebook. "Elizabeth," she said. "Elizabeth Farmer."

Liza waited.

"Your brother was in my class, wasn't he?"

"Yes," said Liza.

"*His* work improved a great deal that year. I am sure yours will too." Mrs. Rumford wrote DO OVER in big red letters on the top of Liza's page.

I don't care, thought Liza. She closed her book. She made a face at Mrs. Rumford's back.

When all the notebooks were checked, Mrs. Rumford said, "There will be no homework today—"

The class cheered.

"Except," said Mrs. Rumford, "for those of you who have DO OVER in your notebooks. I will look at those notebooks first thing in the morning. Now you may line up. Row one first."

Liza was so angry she felt as if she might explode. She grabbed her things and ran to get in line.

"In *this* class we walk," said Mrs. Rumford.

Liza could hardly wait to get away. She could hardly wait to see Heather. She would tell her how terrible Mrs. Rumford was and how much she hated her. Now, if only Mrs. Rumford would hurry up and let them go.

Mrs. Rumford waited until everyone was quiet. Then she opened the door.

Liza pushed forward. She felt someone tap her arm. It was Bridget. But Liza did not wait to talk with her. As soon as she was out of the room, she raced down the hall and ran downstairs and out the door.

Where was Heather?

Liza saw lots of other kids from Mrs. Lane's class. Then she saw Heather. She was walking away from the school.

She was walking with Monica Marks.

7

Liza ran all the way home.

She did not stop when she heard Heather calling her. She did not stop until she reached her own front door. Her chest hurt from running, and her throat felt hot from trying not to cry.

Liza closed the door quietly behind her.

No one was in the living room. Good. She could hear the radio playing, back in the kitchen, and her mother talking with Peggy. Edward was probably not home yet.

Liza tiptoed up the stairs and down the hall to her bedroom. She stepped over Peggy's toys carefully so no one in the kitchen below would hear her. She lay down on her bed.

Then Liza started to cry. Third grade was ruined. Mrs. Lane didn't care. Mrs. Ross, the principal, didn't care. Mrs. Rumford was mean. Everything was terrible. But most of all, Liza cried because Heather was not her real friend.

Liza cried and cried. She cried until she heard a noise in the room.

Liza looked up. Peggy was staring at her.

"Why are you crying?" asked Peggy.

"Go away," yelled Liza. "Get out of here!"

Peggy moved closer. "Were you bad in school? Did you get in trouble?"

"I said, get out of here," Liza shouted.

Peggy didn't move. "I don't have to. It's my room too. And *I* was good in school."

Liza sat up. "You get out of here right now, you little brat." She picked up her lunch box and threw it at Peggy. It crashed into the wall and flew open.

Peggy ran out the door. "Mommy, Mommy," she screamed. "Liza threw her lunch box at me, and she's *crying*!"

Liza could hear Peggy stamp down the stairs and run back to the kitchen. Then she heard the front door slam.

"Hi, Mom. I'm hungry," yelled Edward. "Guess what happened in school?" Edward went back to the kitchen.

Liza waited for her mother to come up and yell at her. Nobody cares about me, she thought. Not even my own family.

Liza looked down at her dress. It was a mess. "I don't care," she said out loud. "I'm never going to wear a dress again in my whole life. That will show them." She lay back down on her bed. She turned her face to the wall.

Where *was* her mother? She doesn't even care enough to come up and yell at me, thought Liza. She's too busy feeding Edward and talking to Peggy.

Then Liza heard someone in the hall. She heard little clicking footsteps on her floor.

It was Chester.

"Good dog," said Liza. "Are you still my friend?"

Chester wagged his tail. He jumped up on Liza's bed.

"You *are* my friend," said Liza. She rubbed her wet face against Chester's furry head. "You are my only friend in the whole world," she told him.

Chester jumped off the bed. He went over to Liza's open lunch box. He found the tuna fish sandwich.

"Hey, stop that, you dumb dog," yelled Liza. She ran over to take the sandwich away from Chester. Chester was too fast. He ran out the door.

Liza started to run after him. She almost ran right into her mother.

"What was that? What did Chester have?" Mrs. Farmer asked.

"My sandwich—from lunch," said Liza.

"Hmmm," said her mother. She came into the room. "Edward says your class was changed, Liza. I'm sorry. Really I am. Tell me what happened."

"No," said Liza. She shook her head.

Liza was surprised at herself. She didn't mean to say no. It just popped out. She looked at her mother.

"It can't be that bad," said Mrs. Farmer kindly. "Maybe I can help."

"No," said Liza again. The only help she wanted was to get out of Mrs. Rumford's class. She knew her mother would never help her do that. Her mother thought Mrs. Rumford was a good teacher. She thought Edward had learned a lot in third grade.

"You know, Liza," said Mrs. Farmer, "Mrs. Rumford is really a very good teacher—"

"I *hate* her," said Liza. "I don't want to talk about her."

Her mother sighed. "Things have a way of working out for the best," she said. She picked up Liza's lunch box.

"No they *don't*," said Liza. "I *hate* Mrs. Rumford."

"Come down when you're ready," said her mother. "I can't talk with you when you won't even listen." Then she left Liza alone.

"I don't care," said Liza to herself. She sat down on her bed. Downstairs the doorbell rang. Probably for Edward. Edward still had some friends. Liza had nobody. She felt tears coming again.

"Liza," her mother called. "It's Heather."

Liza stopped crying. "Tell her I don't want to see her," she called back.

"Too late," said Heather. "I'm here."

8

"Go away," said Liza. "I said I don't want to see you." She got up off the bed.

"Why?" asked Heather. She came into the room. "Why are you mad at me? Why didn't you wait for me after school?"

"What do you *mean*?" yelled Liza. "I *did* wait for you. *You* didn't wait for me. I saw you going off with Monica. Monica with the *beautiful* hair. Monica with the *stupid* face. What kind of a friend are—"

"Wait!" said Heather. "And stop yelling at me. It's not what you think."

"Well?" said Liza. She crossed her arms.

"I was going to wait for you, but—"

"Sure," said Liza. "That's why I saw you walking with Monica." Liza sat down on her bed.

Heather pushed some stuffed animals out of the way. Then she sat down on Peggy's bed. "Monica asked me if I would walk with her just to the end of the block," she said. "Then I was coming back to meet you. Monica said she wanted to tell me something."

Liza made a face. "She probably wanted to tell you how great she is."

"Oh, come on," said Heather. "Monica is okay. She was really nice today."

"Maybe she was nice to *you*," said Liza. "But that's just because *I* wasn't there. She hates me. And I hate her."

Heather picked up one of Peggy's stuffed animals. She held the pink-and-white bear in her lap. "Well, I still think Monica is nice. But let's talk about something else."

"Okay," said Liza. She didn't want to talk

about Monica either. Monica was her enemy. And that was that.

"Heather," she said, "you have to help me think of a way to get out of Mrs. Rumford's class. You can do it. You're smart."

"I'll try," said Heather, "if that's what you want. But is Mrs. Rumford really so terrible? What does she *do*?"

Liza picked up her notebook. She opened it and showed Heather the first page. "That's what she does," she said.

"Wow," said Heather. She put the pink-and-white bear down. She looked at the notebook. "DO OVER. Mrs. Rumford really *is* mean. Does your mother know?"

"She didn't see my notebook," said Liza. "She thinks Mrs. Rumford is a good teacher."

"Poor you," said Heather.

"And guess what else?" said Liza. She took a deep breath. "Mrs. Rumford calls me *Elizabeth*. . . . And I have to sit next to William Spear. . . . And Amy Cutter sits in front of me. . . . And all of our work is boring. . . . And NEATNESS COUNTS." Liza stopped to think of more bad things.

It felt good to tell Heather about how terrible Mrs. Rumford was. It was almost fun.

"Poor you," said Heather again. She stopped. "I think someone is coming upstairs," she said.

Liza listened. "It's my mother." She closed her notebook and sat on it. "I can tell."

"Hello, girls." Mrs. Farmer had a tray in her hands. "I thought you might like a snack. How about some grilled cheese sandwiches and milk?"

Liza's stomach growled. She was starving. She could almost taste those grilled cheese sandwiches. She looked at her mother. Then she looked down. She knew her mother was trying to make her feel better, but Liza was still angry at her for being on Mrs. Rumford's side. She didn't answer.

"I love grilled cheese," said Heather. "Thank you."

Mrs. Farmer put the tray down. She turned to go. Then she stopped. "Do you girls have homework?" she asked.

"No," said Heather. "Not on the first day of school."

Liza didn't want her mother to know about her DO OVER homework. At least not yet. She didn't say anything.

9

"Hurry," said Heather. "Walk faster."

Liza's feet dragged. She couldn't believe it was only the second day of school. At home Peggy could hardly wait to go. And now Heather was in a rush.

"Come *on*," said Heather. She started to walk ahead.

Liza tried to walk faster. Then she remembered her homework. Mrs. Rumford was going to check it right away. Liza had done it quickly last night. She had not shown it to her mother. She hoped it was a little neater than it had been the first time. What if she had to do it all over again?

And over . . . and over . . . and over . . .

This was going to be a very long year. Liza sighed. She walked a little slower.

Now they were at the schoolyard gate.

Heather ran over to the other girls from Mrs. Lane's class.

Liza didn't know what to do.

If she followed Heather, she would have to listen to everybody talking about how great third grade was.

Liza could see Heather talking to Monica Marks. Heather and Monica both had ponytails today. They both had dresses on, too.

Liza was wearing jeans and a yellow T-shirt. She didn't care how she looked for Mrs. Rumford. She reached up and pulled at her hair. It would never be long enough for a ponytail. Never. And she didn't care about that either.

Liza started to walk slowly toward Heather. She tried to look cheerful. She didn't want everyone to know how terrible she felt.

But Heather knew. Heather was going to

help her think of a plan to get back into Mrs. Lane's class.

At least that was what she had said yesterday. But maybe today Heather would change her mind. She looked happy talking with Monica.

The whistle blew. Good. Now Liza didn't have to go over to Heather and Monica.

Everybody was getting in line. Liza walked past Mrs. Lane's class. She did not look. She was afraid some of the kids might be looking at her. Feeling sorry for her.

Liza kept going. She got in line next to Nancy Higgins.

"Hi, Liza," Nancy said. She smiled.

Liza smiled back. Nancy was nice.

More kids were coming. Amy Cutter ran up. She pulled Nancy by the arm. "Come stand with me, Nancy," she said.

Nancy moved back with Amy. She left Liza standing alone.

Liza moved to the end of the line. She

couldn't stay where she was with no one next to her.

The line started moving. Someone ran into Liza from behind. She turned around. It was Bridget Duffy.

Bridget was out of breath. She stepped up next to Liza. "Sorry, Elizabeth," she said. "I was late. I had to run." Bridget was wearing jeans again. And today she had on a red-striped shirt.

"Don't call me Elizabeth," said Liza.

"No talking," called Mrs. Rumford.

Bridget looked at Liza. "Why?" she whispered. "Isn't that your name?"

"Everybody calls me Liza," Liza whispered back. "Everybody except for Mrs. Rumford. She's the meanest teacher in the whole school."

They were almost at their room. The line stopped moving.

"I am hearing a lot of talking," said Mrs. Rumford. "In *this* class we walk quietly in the

halls." She looked back at Bridget and Liza.

Liza closed her mouth in a tight line. So did Bridget.

Mrs. Rumford turned around. The line began to move again.

Liza started laughing. She looked at Bridget. Bridget was laughing too. They both put their hands over their mouths so Mrs. Rumford would not hear them.

"Bridget," Liza whispered. "Will you eat lunch with me today?"

"Okay, *Liza,*" said Bridget. She smiled.

They went into the classroom together. Liza felt almost happy.

10

Liza stood at Mrs. Rumford's desk.

"Elizabeth," said Mrs. Rumford. "This is *not* good work." She pointed to Liza's messy notebook.

Liza didn't say anything. She knew it was not good work. She crossed her fingers behind her back. Please, she thought. Don't make me do it all over again. Please . . .

"I won't ask you to do this homework again," Mrs. Rumford was saying. "But next time—"

"Thank you, Mrs. Rumford." Liza grabbed her notebook. She started to run back to her desk.

"Walk!" said Mrs. Rumford.

Liza slid into her seat. That was close. Too close. She looked around. There was a big list of spelling words to copy from the board. Amy Cutter was working hard. William Spear was blowing his nose. Bridget was biting her fingernail. She took her hand out of her mouth and smiled at Liza.

Liza smiled back. Then she started to work. All around her, pencils were scratching away. Everyone was busy.

Suddenly, Mrs. Rumford stood up.

Everyone stopped working.

"I have some good news," said Mrs. Rumford.

Liza sat up straight. What could it be?

Mrs. Rumford waited until everyone was quiet.

"Almost all of you do very neat printing," she said. "The kind of work I like to see in this class."

Was that the news? It didn't sound like good news to Liza. It didn't sound like anything.

"I know it is only the second day of school," Mrs. Rumford went on. "But I think that most of you are ready to learn to write in script."

Script! That really was good news. Wonderful news. Liza was the only one in her family who couldn't write script. Except for Peggy. And Peggy didn't count. She couldn't write anything.

Liza could almost feel her hand making those fancy looping letters. And her name would be beautiful in script. Elizabeth—not Liza. Elizabeth was nice and long. Liza could hardly wait to get started. Maybe, she thought, they would start right away.

Amy Cutter raised her hand. "When are we—"

"Finish your spelling words, and your math worksheets," said Mrs. Rumford. "If we *all* work hard this morning, we can start script after lunch."

Great, thought Liza. Probably Mrs. Lane's class wouldn't learn script for a long time. She hoped not.

Liza picked up her pencil. She started working. *Pop*. The pencil point broke.

Liza raised her hand. "Mrs. Rumford, my pencil—"

"*Some* of us," said Mrs. Rumford, "*some* of us will need to work harder than others."

Liza sharpened her pencil. She started working again. She finished all of the spelling words and her math worksheet. Everything was as neat as could be. She sat back to rest.

Amy Cutter raised her hand. "I'm all finished," she said.

"Good," said Mrs. Rumford. "Who else has finished?"

Liza put her hand up. So did some of the other kids.

"I need to find out where we are in reading," Mrs. Rumford went on. "I will read with you one at a time. The rest of you may draw if your work is done. And you may talk quietly."

Mrs. Rumford chose Amy to give out

drawing paper. Amy went around to every desk.

Liza looked at the piece of paper Amy had given her. It was yellow around the edge. Probably left over from five years ago. Amy probably gave herself a good piece from the middle of the stack.

"Amy," said Mrs. Rumford. "You may read with me first."

Teacher's pet, said Liza to herself.

As soon as Amy was away from her desk, Liza reached out and grabbed her drawing paper. She put her own yellow piece on Amy's desk. Would Amy know what had happened? Too bad if she did. She couldn't prove it.

Liza looked around. Everybody was drawing or doing math. No one had seen her.

She took her crayons out of her desk. She knew just what she wanted to draw. A picture of Mrs. Lane. It would be beautiful. She would give it to Mrs. Lane after school. Mrs. Lane would be so happy she would ask the

70

principal to let Liza come back to her class. She could see it all. It would be great.

Liza felt someone tapping her arm.

"Hey, Liza, can I borrow some crayons?" It was Bridget.

Liza pointed to her box. "You can share," she said.

"Thanks," said Bridget. "I'm going to make a design. What about you?"

Liza looked at her blank page. Suddenly her idea seemed silly. Mrs. Lane would say thank you if she gave her a picture. And that would be that. Besides, she didn't know how to draw people very well. "I guess I'll make a design too," she said.

When it was Liza's turn to read, she went up to sit next to Mrs. Rumford. Liza was a good reader, but she hated to read out loud. It made her feel nervous, and she always made dumb mistakes.

Mrs. Rumford pointed to a page in a green reader. "Try this," she said.

It was the same reader Liza had last year. Liza started to read. It was easy.

Mrs. Rumford closed the book. She opened a yellow one. "Now try this one," she said.

Liza looked. Not so easy. She read a few sentences slowly.

Mrs. Rumford said, "You will be in the yellow book. I think you can do it. Take one from the shelf."

Liza got up. She took a yellow book. She looked around. Nancy had a green book. Joseph had a blue one. Blue was really easy. But Amy had a yellow book, and so did William Spear. That meant Amy and William would be in her group. Yuck.

Liza went back to her seat.

"Bridget Duffy," called Mrs. Rumford.

"Good luck," said Liza, as Bridget headed for the front of the room.

Liza watched Mrs. Rumford. First she opened the green book. Bridget read so quietly that Liza couldn't hear her.

Mrs. Rumford closed the green book. She opened the yellow one.

Good, thought Liza. At least if she had to be in the same group as Amy and William, Bridget would be in it too.

But she was wrong.

Mrs. Rumford said something to Bridget. Bridget nodded. Then she came back to her desk. She did not have a book from the shelf.

"How come you—?" started Liza.

Amy Cutter turned around too. "Why didn't you get a book?" she said.

Bridget looked embarrassed. "Mrs. Rumford said I should read on my own. Library books."

"What?" said Amy.

"I'm a pretty good reader," said Bridget quietly.

Amy gave her a nasty look. "Big deal," she said. Then she turned back around.

Bridget sighed. "That's what happened at my old school," she said. "Kids thought I was showing off just because I'm a good reader."

"Not me," said Liza. "I don't think you're showing off."

"Really?" said Bridget.

"Really," said Liza. She wondered how she could get to be as good a reader as Bridget. It would be great to just read library books. No more readers. No more reading out loud in a group. She had never thought about it before. Readers and workbooks were just a part of school, like math and spelling and other boring things. But now . . . If Bridget could read on her own, maybe other people could too. Like me, thought Liza.

"Would you like to come to my house someday after school?" Bridget said. "I could ask my mother."

"Yes," said Liza. "And you can come to my house too, if you want to."

"I do want to," said Bridget. She started to work on her design again. She looked happy.

Liza thought about Bridget. She wondered what her house was like, and what they would do there. Maybe they would read library books together. Maybe they would be friends.

But what about Heather? Would she like Bridget too?

11

It was time to go home. Everyone got in line. Everyone except Liza. She waited until the others were gone. Then she went up to Mrs. Rumford's desk. She had been thinking about a plan all afternoon. It seemed like a good idea. Now she just had to ask Mrs. Rumford.

Mrs. Rumford was working on some papers. "Did you want to talk to me, Elizabeth?" she asked.

Liza nodded. "It's about my reader." She stopped.

"Yes?" said Mrs. Rumford.

Liza started again. "You said I'm going to be in the yellow reader. . . ."

"Yes," said Mrs. Rumford. "I know that the yellow book is going to be a bit hard, Elizabeth. But I feel sure that you can manage it."

"No," said Liza.

Mrs. Rumford looked surprised.

Liza felt herself get red. "I mean, that's not what I was going to say."

Mrs. Rumford waited.

Liza took a deep breath. "I was wondering if I could take the yellow reader home . . . do extra work. I . . . I want to be a good reader." There, she'd said it.

"Well," said Mrs. Rumford. "I am very pleased to hear that you have such an interest in your schoolwork, Elizabeth. I must say I'm quite surprised. But as far as your reading goes, you are doing third-grade work. You don't need to take your reader home." Mrs. Rumford looked back down at her papers.

"But I *want* to," said Liza. She had to make

Mrs. Rumford see that she really wanted to read better. *"Please."*

"Elizabeth, if I let you take your reader home, how will you be able to work in a group at school? No, I don't think this is a good idea." She shook her head.

Liza thought about the yellow group, Amy Cutter and William Spear, and . . . "It will be okay," she said quickly. "I don't need to work in a group. My mother can help me at home. And Bridget is not in a group. She can help me at school."

Liza hoped Bridget wouldn't mind.

"Hmmm," said Mrs. Rumford.

Liza crossed her fingers. She tried to cross her toes, but her sneakers were too tight. "Please," she said. "I'll work extra hard."

"I can see that this means a lot to you, Elizabeth. And, of course, I like to see someone who is willing to work hard. . . ."

Liza held her breath.

"I suppose we can try it," said Mrs. Rumford. "On one condition."

81

"Oh, thank you, Mrs. Rumford. Thank you." Liza was so happy she felt like dancing around the room.

"The condition is," Mrs. Rumford went on, "that you must keep up with your other schoolwork."

"I can do it," said Liza. "I know I can." She tried not to think about math worksheets. She wasn't at all sure she could keep up with those.

"I think you can do it, too, Elizabeth." Mrs. Rumford smiled.

Liza said thank you again, before Mrs. Rumford had time to change her mind. Then she turned and ran out of the room.

"Walk," Mrs. Rumford called.

But Liza ran down the stairs and out the door.

She hoped Heather was still waiting for her.

She looked around. Yes, there was Heather, talking with Monica Marks, of course.

Liza ran over to them. She could hardly wait to tell Heather about her day. Script, and no more reading groups, and her new friend, Bridget. Third grade was not going to be so bad after all.

"Heather," she said, "guess what?"

"What took you so long?" Heather asked. "I thought you left without me."

"I wouldn't do that," said Liza. "I was with Mrs. Rumford, and guess what?"

Monica touched Heather's arm. "Bye," she said. "I'll see you tomorrow. Don't forget about the party on Friday."

"What party?" said Liza. She didn't like the funny way Monica and Heather were looking at her.

"I'll tell you later," said Heather quickly.

"My birthday party," said Monica. She smiled at Liza. Not a nice smile. "It's going to be at my house," she said. "For some of my friends from Mrs. Lane's class."

Liza felt sick. She felt as if Monica had punched her in the stomach. She couldn't talk.

"Bye," said Monica. "I'll see you tomorrow."

Liza watched her walk away, her long ponytail swinging as she walked.

"It's okay if I go, isn't it, Liza?" Heather asked.

Liza didn't answer.

"Liza," said Heather. "I *have* to go to her party. All the girls in the class are going."

Liza still didn't say anything.

"And besides," Heather went on, "I *like* Monica. She's my friend."

Finally Liza could talk. "If she's your friend, you can walk to school with her. Because I'm never going to be your friend again. Never."

Liza started to walk away.

"Oh, come on, Liza," said Heather. She started walking too. "You know you're my best friend. And besides, I can't walk to school with Monica. She lives the other way."

"Too bad," said Liza. She kept walking. She would not look at Heather. Heather might see that she was about to cry.

"*I* wouldn't care if *you* were friends with

84

someone in Mrs. Rumford's class," said Heather. "*I* would understand."

Liza thought about Bridget. She remembered that she was going to go to Bridget's house. But that was different. Not the same at all.

When they got to Liza's house, Liza opened her door. "I hope you have fun at the stupid party," she said. "And I hope you like walking to school alone." Then she went in and slammed the door.

12

"Liza," said Mrs. Farmer. "Eat your breakfast. Heather will be here any minute."

Liza stared at her cornflakes. She wasn't hungry.

Maybe I'm sick, she thought. Too sick to go to school. She did not tell her mother that Heather wasn't coming. That she might never come again.

Liza tried to think about something else. She remembered her homework. She had done all of it last night, *and* she had read three stories in her reader. Some of the words were hard, but her mother had helped. She had been happy when Liza told her about the extra reading at home.

And Liza thought the stories were pretty good. She was sure she would be reading library books in no time at all.

Liza started to eat her cornflakes.

"I don't want to go to school today."

Liza couldn't believe her ears. She looked up from her cereal. It was Peggy.

Edward and Mrs. Farmer were looking at Peggy too.

No one said anything.

"I'm going to stay home," said Peggy. She stared back at them.

"But Peggy, what's the matter?" said her mother. "I thought you *liked* school. I thought you *liked* being a big girl."

"Not anymore," said Peggy. She took a spoonful of cereal. Milk dribbled down her chin.

"Did you get in trouble yesterday?" asked Liza. "Was someone mean to you?"

"No," said Peggy. "I just want to stay home today. And tomorrow too, maybe."

"Wow!" said Edward. "First it's Liza, and now it's Peggy. School's not so bad, once you get used to it."

"Ha!" said Liza. "You were the one who was saying third grade was terrible."

"Well," said Edward, "third grade *is* terrible if you have Mrs. Rumford. But everyone knows kindergarten is fun."

"I'm *not* going," said Peggy.

Mrs. Farmer reached over and felt Peggy's forehead. "Cool," she said. "No fever. If you're not sick, you have to go to school."

"No," said Peggy. She started to cry.

"Oh dear," said her mother.

Edward finished his juice. "I'm going. Got to meet the guys." He pushed his chair back. "Listen, Peggy," he said. "You've got to go to school so you can grow up to be big and smart—like me."

"Oh, get out of here," said Liza. But Edward was already gone.

Peggy was still crying.

"*Something* must have happened yesterday to make you so upset, Peggy," said Mrs. Farmer. "If you tell us, maybe we can help you."

"No," cried Peggy.

"Come on, Peggy," said Liza. "School isn't so bad. It's really okay."

Peggy sniffed. "No it's not. *You* said you hate school."

"That was a mistake," Liza said quickly. "There are lots of good things about school."

"Like what?" said Peggy. She sniffed again. But at least she was listening.

Liza thought about how angry she had been when she got Mrs. Rumford instead of Mrs. Lane. She thought about how Mrs. Rumford called her Elizabeth, and wrote DO OVER on her homework. She thought about Heather and Monica being friends.

Liza looked at Peggy. "Well," she said. "You learn how to read in school, and write."

"Not in kindergarten," said Peggy. She

started to cry again. "All we do is baby stuff."

"Oh, no, Peggy," said her mother. "You will learn lots of things in kindergarten."

"No," said Peggy. "I asked the teacher when we would get reading books. She said I had to wait until first grade. And Ronni and Amanda laughed at me. And I'm never going back."

It's true, thought Liza. Kindergarten isn't all fun. She knew just how Peggy must feel.

"Peggy," said her mother. "I'm sure you will have a lot of fun in kindergarten. Your teacher is really very nice. Maybe if I talk to her—"

"No!" screamed Peggy. "Don't talk to her. Don't."

"Liza," said her mother. "You'd better get ready. Heather will be here any minute."

Liza got up from the table. She didn't say that Heather wasn't coming. That Heather was not her friend anymore.

Peggy was still crying. Now her nose was running too.

"Peggy," Liza said. "Your teacher forgot to tell you about . . ." Liza thought quickly. "About worksheets."

"Worksheets?" said Peggy.

"Yes," said Liza. "In kindergarten you don't get reading books. But you *do* get worksheets." Liza crossed her fingers. She hoped Peggy's teacher would give worksheets. She was pretty sure that all kindergarten kids did them.

"What are they?" asked Peggy.

"Well," said Liza, "you have to do stuff . . . like draw lines and count things and put circles around the right answer. It's very . . . important."

"Worksheets," said Peggy to herself.

"I'll bet the other kids in your class don't know about worksheets," said Liza. "You're probably the only kid in the whole kindergarten who knows."

"Really?" said Peggy. "Maybe I could tell Ronni and Amanda."

"Peggy," said her mother. "If you want to

talk to Ronni and Amanda, you'd better finish your breakfast so we can go to school."

"But—" said Peggy. "I don't—"

"Peggy," said Liza. "You can walk with me today, if you want to."

"Really?" said Peggy.

"Just today," warned Liza. "Not every day."

"Liza, that's very nice of you," said her mother.

Peggy started to run out of the kitchen. "Good-bye, Mommy."

"Stop," said her mother. "You need a good-bye kiss. Both of you." She kissed Peggy, and Peggy ran out of the room.

Then she kissed Liza. "Thank you," she said, "for being such a good big sister."

"That's okay," said Liza. "I guess kindergarten can be terrible sometimes too. Just like third grade."

Liza headed for the front door. She wished Heather would be there waiting for her.

Liza had an extra orange in her lunch box to share with Bridget. She had her script homework and her new yellow reader. But without Heather to talk to, none of these things seemed special.

Liza opened the door.

Peggy was waiting outside. "Heather isn't here yet," she said.

"Come on," said Liza. "Today we're going to walk to school alone."

13

Liza had to take Peggy to her classroom.

She looked around the schoolyard quickly as they walked past. She saw Heather and Monica talking with some other girls. Liza hoped they wouldn't see her. She tried to hurry.

Suddenly Peggy stopped walking. "Look," she said. "There's Heather."

"Come on, Peggy," said Liza. She grabbed Peggy's hand and pulled her along. "You don't want to be late, do you?"

"But Liza—"

Liza pulled harder. She didn't stop until they

were inside the school at the kindergarten door.

"Bye, Peggy," she said. Then she ran down the hall and into the girls' room. She could stay there until it was time to go to her classroom. She couldn't go out to the yard alone. She just couldn't.

Soon the hall was filled with noise. Footsteps and talking, and doors opening and closing.

Liza pushed open the bathroom door a crack. She waited until she saw her class. Then she got on the end of the line next to Bridget.

"Hi," said Bridget. "Why weren't you out in the yard? I was waiting for you."

"I had to bring my sister to her room."

"Oh," said Bridget. "I asked my mother if you could come to my house after school someday. And she said yes. Can you come on Friday?"

"I think so," said Liza. "I'll ask my mother."

They were at the top of the stairs. The line stopped moving.

"Who is talking back there?" called Mrs. Rumford.

Everyone got quiet.

Mrs. Rumford walked back toward Liza and Bridget. "Were you the ones who were talking?"

Liza looked at her shoes.

Bridget didn't answer either.

"I cannot have this noise in the halls," said Mrs. Rumford. "Both of you will walk quietly downstairs. Then you may come back up again. You can meet the rest of us in our room."

Liza and Bridget turned around. They started back down the stairs.

"And," said Mrs. Rumford, "I don't want to hear a peep from either one of you. Not a single peep." Mrs. Rumford closed the stairwell door.

"Peep," said Liza very quietly. "Peep, peep."

"Peep," answered Bridget, *not* so quietly.

And then they were both peeping and laughing at the same time.

"In *this* class," said Liza, in her best Mrs. Rumford voice, "we will have no peeping. Not a single peep."

"Liza," said Bridget. "What do you think she'd do if we never came back? If we just kept going?"

"That would be great," said Liza. "Except that I already did all of my homework for today. I don't want to waste it."

"I did mine too," said Bridget.

"Too bad," said Liza. "Maybe next time."

"Peep," said Bridget.

Mrs. Rumford stopped talking when Liza and Bridget quietly entered the room. "That's much better, girls," she said.

She waited for them to sit down. Then she started talking again about the morning work.

Liza looked over at Bridget. Bridget was

really nice. It would be fun to go to her house after school on Friday.

Friday!

That was the day Monica Marks was having her birthday party. The party that Heather was going to.

Liza was sorry she had yelled at Heather. She missed her a lot. They had been best friends for a long time.

I should never have said those things to her, Liza thought. Now she's not my friend, and it's my own fault.

"Elizabeth, are you paying attention?" said Mrs. Rumford.

"Yes," said Liza. She sat up straight. She tried to listen to Mrs. Rumford. But she couldn't. She kept thinking about Heather.

She had to tell Heather she was sorry. Tell her that it was okay about the party.

But when? She didn't want to do it when Heather was with Monica.

Mrs. Rumford finished talking. She sat down at her desk.

Everyone started working. Liza didn't know what she was supposed to do. She didn't care. The more she thought about Heather, the worse she felt.

She just had to do something now. She couldn't wait. Liza slipped out of her seat. She went up to the teacher's desk.

"Mrs. Rumford, I need to leave the room."

Mrs. Rumford frowned. "Already, Elizabeth?"

"Yes," said Liza.

"Well, go ahead then," said Mrs. Rumford. "But please be quick."

Liza hurried out of the classroom. She knew Mrs. Rumford thought she was going to the bathroom, and that was fine with her.

She ran down the hall to Mrs. Lane's room. Liza took a deep breath. Then she opened the door.

Mrs. Lane was writing on the board, but she stopped when Liza came in.

Liza walked over to her. "I need to talk to

Heather," she said quietly. "In the hall. It's very important. Please."

Mrs. Lane looked surprised. "Liza, we're right in the middle of a lesson," she said. "I'm sure you can wait until lunchtime."

Everybody was looking at Liza. She felt terrible. How could she have done such a dumb thing? Everybody must be thinking how dumb she was. Liza felt tears coming. "I'm sorry . . ." she said to Mrs. Lane. "I . . ." Liza turned to leave the room.

"Wait, Liza," said Mrs. Lane. "Heather can go. But just for a moment. Heather," she said, "will you please go with Liza?"

"Thank you," said Liza. She turned and walked out of the room.

Heather followed her. "What do you want, Liza?" she said. "Why are you here?"

"I couldn't wait," said Liza. "I had to tell you I'm sorry. And it's okay if you go to the party." Liza stopped.

Heather looked at her. "Are you crazy?"

she said. "You got me out of the room to tell me *that*? What did you say to Mrs. Rumford?"

"She thinks I'm in the bathroom," said Liza.

Heather smiled. "I'm glad you're not mad at me anymore," she said.

Mrs. Lane opened the door. "Finish up, girls. One more minute." She closed the door.

"She's so nice," said Heather. "I wish you were still in our room."

"Me too," said Liza. "But it's really not so bad in Mrs. Rumford's class."

There were so many things that Liza wanted to tell Heather about—script, and reading on her own, and her new friend, Bridget. But they could wait, now that she and Heather were friends again.

"I have to go," said Liza.

"Bye," said Heather. "See you after school." She went into her room.

Liza started back toward her class. She felt wonderful.

She hoped they would work on script this morning, or maybe reading. But even if it was math, she was ready. She skipped down the hall and pushed open her door. Third grade was going to be great.